VIKING KESTREL
Published by the Penguin Group
Viking Penguin Inc., 40 West 23rd Street, New York, New York 10010, U.S.A.
Penguin Books Ltd, 27 Wrights Lane, London W8 5TZ, England
Penguin Books Australia Ltd, Ringwood, Victoria, Australia
Penguin Books Canada Ltd, 2801 John Street, Markham, Ontario, Canada L3R 1B4
Penguin Books (N.Z.) Ltd, 182–190 Wairau Road, Auckland 10, New Zealand

Penguin Books Ltd, Registered Offices: Harmondsworth, Middlesex, England

First published in 1989 by Viking Penguin Inc.

Published simultaneously in Canada

1 3 5 7 9 10 8 6 4 2

Text copyright © Harriet Ziefert, 1989

Illustrations copyright © Deborah Kogan Ray, 1989

All rights reserved

Library of Congress catalog card number: 88-51465

ISBN 0-670-82749-5

Printed in Singapore for Harriet Ziefert, Inc.

New Boots For Spring

A BOOK OF SEASONS

By Harriet Ziefert & Deborah Kogan Ray

VIKING KESTREL

Now it's spring.
See my new umbrella.
See my new raincoat.
See my new boots.

See my pail.
See my shovel.

Look what I can do.
I can make mud pies.

I can pick flowers.
I smell tulips.

Then it's summer.
See my new shorts.
See my new hat.

See my sandbox.
See my dump truck.
See my sunglasses.

Look what I can do.
I can find ants.

I can splash.
Splishity splash!
It's hot!

Then it's fall.
See my new sweater.
See my new hat.
See my red wagon.

See my big rake.
Look what I can do.
I can fall down in the leaves.

I can feel the wind.
I can watch the birds.
Good-bye, birds.

Then it's winter.
See my new mittens.
See my new scarf.
See my new hat.

See my sled.
See my snowboots.

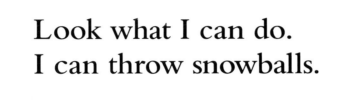

Look what I can do.
I can throw snowballs.

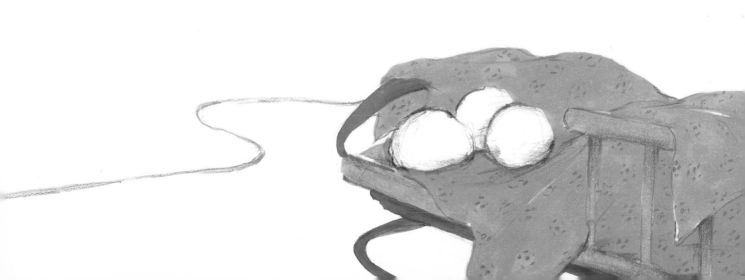

I can taste icicles.
Lickety lick!
It's cold!